I look up to you.

Not only have you
outlasted sorrows
you've remained
strong enough
to reach out
with interest
in another person.

Your interest
in these words
is a gift for me.

For a long time
the thought of us together
has animated me
with a sense of
great beauty.
That beauty,
that miracle of beauty,
is the gift
of you.

Because I respect you
my main purpose in life
is to try to live up
to you.

My respect for you
makes me hope
I can meet you
in a place
where we share
pleasure and understanding.

It's a place where I want
to be with you
to honor
and comfort you.

It's where I feel
your greatness
makes everything
turn out for the best.

-Steve Jackson

Los Angeles Poets Press
since 1983
Copyright 2020 Steve Jackson
2nd Edition
ISBN 9780578 790749
Library of Congress
Control Number
2014905336

stevejacksonpoems.com

In the short time we have in eternity
the purpose of life is to live
and to live is to love.

Facundo Cabral

Forward

*Embark
on a powerful journey
through the darkness
into the beauty
and peace
of the light.*

Told with poignant, passionate prose
that seems like conversational poetry
reflecting universal themes
of love, life, sorrow, joy and gratitude,
An Affair in the Valley
forms a powerful and moving testament
to the world with her great people.

Echoing author Steve Jackson's journey
through hardship and darkness,
this exquisite collection explores both
the dark and the light,
from sorrow to rapture,
and his ascent to a place of peace.

Steve sees the light
because he's felt the darkness,
living for months out of his pickup
with no end in sight. But through this,
his mind was liberated and delivered
to witness the beauty of life
around him, a life where people
climb from sorrow's abyss
to stand on love's common ground,
the world, home in the stars.

An Affair in the Valley

A Collection of Poems

Contents

Rupi

When fear tries
to chain me down in darkness
I think about Rupi Kaur.

She writes books.

Though I don't know her personally
I feel I know her
from the books she's written.

With her sincere,
intelligent
friendly words
she lifts me
out of darkness.

She shows her own heart
scarred and healing
and I admire her strength
to endure.

I admire her beautiful honesty
showing it's wisdom
to love and confide.

With her noble ideals
she gives the world a good person
lighting the road ahead
like the warm sun
after a cold night.

Her glowing words
paint pictures
fresh from life
and bring home to my heart
the truth
they spring out of.

Her pure intention
to love without guile
makes me want to protect her
from anything that might hurt her.

I admire you, Rupi.

Where fear
can chain a soul
you break off the chain
and walk in freedom
with a new person
in a universe
you turn into
a welcoming home.

Forever

When you hold my hand
I feel touched
by the most graceful person
in the human race.

When you pull me
close to you
I feel you blessing me
with my soul's purest ceremony.

In each other's arms
I feel linked
to the moral truth
of what I'm supposed to do.
I'm supposed to love you.

Your smile
rcnews my scarred heart
and sets it in tune with life.

Your sincere kiss
is love saying
good
is eternal.

Jumper

My Dad and I picked him
out of a litter at the animal shelter.
He was probably a sheepdog.

When he was a puppy
he could jump off the floor
into my lap.
We named him Jumper.

And he could run, too.
He was fast.
I loved to watch him run.
He'd spot the school bus
and run to meet me,
his black and white fur rippling.

He was loving and affectionate,
not vain at all.
There was no guile in him.
And he showed me an example
of social success,
be happy to see people.

Of all his great talents
the one loved most
was his speed
and his love of speed
when he ran so fast
his legs blurred underneath him.

Then there was his compassion.
When I suffered at school
I'd come home and he'd be there
loving me.

And he was a protector.
I'd been swimming in a pond
and when I climbed out of the water
a rattlesnake coiled up
there on the bank.

Turning to retreat fast
back into the water
I saw a blur leaping
like some kind of spirit
landing on the sand
between me and the snake.

It was Jumper
attacking and killing
and getting bit.

It's no wonder some philosopher said,
"The domestication of the dog
is the greatest feat
of the human race."

I held my dog in my arms
while Mom drove us to the vet
and in a few days he was back running,
running fast,
running fast, fast across the field,
meeting me when I got home
from being taught civilization in school.
I felt him, his nose and face in my hand,
his tongue licking me.

Freedom

Life loves freedom.
Birds call out to it.
Trees wave their hands to it.
Dogs yip running to it.

Children joined
on their mutual quest
for joy and love
reach for it
even when
tears of sorrow
can make children feel
wrecked for eternity.

With brilliant resiliency
they are prophets for freedom
reaching out
again and again
joyfully prophesying
love for the way things are.

A Mother's Heart

Some say a mother's heart
is full of love.
Some say it's full of
ambivalence.

My mother's seventy.
She still tells me
she loves me.
She still scowls
and tells me to sit up straight
when I slouch.

And she's still anxious
for me to make a good impression
on her friends.
Her friend Fran is having us
over for dinner tonight
and Fran's custom is for each person
to tell a story after dinner.

Yesterday Mom asked me
if I had a story for Fran
so I told my Mother this story.

In a shop by the street
a shoe repairman takes in
a mute homeless man
and teaches the man
how to repair shoes.

The shoe repairman thinks
the man can't talk
until one day
the man tells him,
"I was an angel in heaven
before God sent me
to the earth."

"Why did you leave heaven?"

"I was ordered to take a child
to heaven
ending the child's life here.
I refused to take the child
and God sent me down
to learn the pain of life on Earth."

When I got to this point in the story
my mother looked impatient.
I could see
the story didn't go over with her.

With a shy look
like she was afraid
of hurting my feelings,
she said, "That's good
but why don't you tell a story
about Fran?
Fran's the friend I've known longest."

To please my mother
I told her another story.

I have an old memory of Fran.
It's a memory I'll never forget.
I was twelve or thirteen
wading in a lake
and playing with her children.

Fran was sitting
in a lawn chair on the sandy beach
with a book in her lap.

Fran was different
from other adults.
She looked at me
like she respected me
and wasn't supervising me.

We talked there by the water.
I told her
one of my first philosophical thoughts,
"It seems like
we all crucify each other."

With a tone of appreciation
for my thought
she said, "If we crucify each other,
then with love
we raise each other from the dead."

One of my strongest memories
from childhood
is Fran looking through sunglasses
over the water
talking about love
raising people
from the dead.

I looked at my mother
to see what she thought.

"Is that it?" she asked.

"Yes."

"Not much of a plot,
but Fran
is better than
the fallen angel."

Part of Me

Waking early before the sunrise
I feel your gentle fingers on my skin
before I realize you're not here.

It makes me smile to remember
you live nearby
and we're within each others' reach.

Leaving the house
to go to work
in the chilly darkness
I zip up my jacket
and feel I'm keeping us both warm,
you're so much a part of me.

And I know you'll be part of
whatever I do or say today.
The way beautiful thoughts
are part of a person's body,
you'll be part of me.

If anybody says anything
encouraging or inspiring to me
I'll feel they're praising us both.

If I were walking alone through darkness
on the other side of the world
I'd still feel us walking close together
discovering a new day
where my dreams would include you
as surely as the sky includes the stars.

And as surely as the sun,
the star for the world,
begins to shine on the street ahead
I know that when I smile today
people will see your smile on my face.

The Garment

My friend Jim told me
he goes back and forth
from loving people
to hating people.

With a look of guilt
he said he wished
he could love people
all the time.
Then he said with a firm voice,
like he was setting his mind
on climbing up a steep, icy trail,
"Words should be
the clothes of love."

With a preachy tone
I told him,
"That's a noble goal,
to make words the clothes of love.
How about making words
the clothes of love
and wisdom?"

He spotted the phony self righteousness
in my voice
and I'm sure
he felt morally superior to me
for my condescending to him.

He'd found me out.
People are smart.
They sense what you think.
They hear it in your tone.
They see it in your eyes.

I apologized saying,
"I'm sorry
if I sounded like I was
preaching to you.
I like your phrase
'Words should be
the clothes of love.'
Could we say 'garments of love'
and give it a bit of flair?"

He said, "Yes,
'garments of love is good,"
and then he went further
with the idea saying,
"Not only words,
people themselves
should be garments of love."

"Well said," I told him,
and we parted on a good note.

Later that night
walking holding hands with my girlfriend
we looked up at the moon and stars.

I asked her,
"Do you ever feel
the moon and stars
are like garments of love?"

And she said,
"Existence itself
is a garment of love."

The Mower

My neighbor Roy is eighty.
His wife died three years ago,
cancer.
He's mourning.
They were married fifty-five years.

After she died
he stayed home,
didn't go anywhere,
sat in his chair
in his living room
and slept all day
everyday.

He went to a social worker
for grief counseling.
She told him,
"Get out into life.
Do something,
or stay there
and die alone
in that chair
in your living room."

So he started doing
volunteer work
delivering meals
to the elderly
and he helps people
here in the neighborhood.
Roy mows the grass
for one of our neighbors, Bill.
Bill has Parkinson's disease.

The other day
I told Roy, "That's nice of you
to mow Bill's grass,"
and Roy said, "It's a hard lawn
because Bill's mower
doesn't have much power in the wheels
and I have to push it.
It's not like my mower.
My mower's got so much power
in the wheels
it almost pulls you
over the grass."

"Why don't you
use your own mower
on Bill's grass?" I asked him.

Roy scowled at me.

"Does my question
deserve your scowl, Roy?"
I asked him with a playful tone.

Though he's twenty years older than I am
we have a playful relationship.
He calls me "lad."

He bowed his head
like he was struggling
with something.

"My mower
was my wife's mower," he said.
"She liked to mow our grass.
She loved that mower.
She always kept it clean and shiny.
I don't want to mow
somebody else's grass with it."

"It has a place
in your heart,"
I told him.

"Yeah," he said
covering his eyes.

Childbirth

My best friend Jim
was worried.
All of us were worried.
His wife was having trouble
in labor.

Friends gathered around him
in the hospital waiting room.

With deep worry lines on his face
he'd softly say, "No thank you,"
when somebody offered
to get him something.
We all felt inadequate
to ease his mind.

Finally the doctor came out
telling Jim his wife and new son
were fine.

Jim wept and hugged the happy doctor
and everybody celebrated later
at Jim's house,
friends and neighbors laughing and toasting,
people passing cigars around.

I sat by Jim on the couch.
He confided to me that he'd lost sight
of religion in college,
but he'd said a prayer in the hospital
for his wife and child.
He said he'd prayed to God
and it made him feel religious again
to know his wife and baby are both safe.

He sipped a glass of wine
and I smiled feeling his happiness.

With a troubled look
he said his childhood religious beliefs
had been shadowed by science
and the size and age
of the universe.
"This universe has been around
a long time,
and it'll be around a lot longer.
We're here at the meeting place
between two eternities,
and why?"

"Maybe life is why," I told him,
and he said, "Yes I guess I should feel
grateful for life.
Maybe this incessant dissatisfaction
with my ignorance
is like a child saying,
'Dad I like my new bike,
but I wish I knew how it works.'"

"Yes," I told him,
"maybe our human race
is like a dog
finding a book on the beach
and giving it the sniff test."

"Yes," he said, "and maybe we humans
should be thankful we know what galaxies are
so we know more than a dog."

"Yes," I told him. "Then again,
maybe all creatures have their own brand
of happiness.
Maybe the dog
is happier than we are.
He doesn't puzzle over things.
He's happy sniffing and yipping,
running at play on the beach,
swimming in the ocean."

We both laughed
and I told him,
"Speaking of new bikes,
I want to buy your son his first bike
if it's alright with you."

"Yes," he said, "when the boy
is old enough. I don't want him
to start riding too young
and fall off.
He'll be suffering enough in his life."

We laughed and Jim said,
"According to Buddha,
suffering is an error in existence."

"Yes I've heard that
suffering is an error in existence,
but if we were happy all the time,
happy would lose its meaning."

"Yes," he said, "the pain
produces the pleasure…
Maybe wondering why
life makes people suffer
is like a child telling his Dad,
'I like my new bike,
but people skin their knees
falling from bikes.'"

"Yes," I told him,
"I've been skinning my knees
since childhood.
When I was a child
I wanted to be a hero.
As I grew older
the hero became a dream
I reached for and couldn't grasp.
I'd become an ordinary guy
falling off a bike."

"Well," said Jim,
"you can get back on.
You can love somebody
and become the idol of your idol."

"Yes I guess so," I said
thinking about my girlfriend.
She was working
and I felt an urge to call her.

Alone in Jim's bedroom
I called her and told her,
"You're my idol."
She laughed and said she got off work early
and was on her way to Jim's.

When she got there
she hugged Jim
and congratulated him.
Everybody toasted the new baby.
One of our friends came up
with a cigar and lit it for Jim.

Jim took a puff
and started coughing violently.

Everybody laughed.

That's Jim.
I've seen him do that before.
It's his way of joking,
coughing like that
after puffing on a cigar.
That's Jim,
pretending to cough
to get a laugh.

And what better gift in this universe
where two eternities meet,
a good laugh.

A World of Love

You know me.

I've told you
about my past.

Before we met
life had wounded me
making me wary.

Then we met.

With your tender insight
you peered into me.

You saw my scarred soul.

I saw your compassion in your eyes,
your compassion filling me
with tender warmth and desire for you.

But I'd rather you don't love me
out of compassion for me.
How can you feel compassion for me now?
You make me happier
than I've ever been.
I'd rather you love me
for discovering with you
a world of love.

An Affair in the Valley

I knew Mary back home
in the valley where we grew up.

She was my classmate
in public school,
and we were classmates
in confirmation class
at the Presbyterian Church
we attended with our families.

In confirmation class
when the minister questioned me
about my faith in Jesus
I tried to give him the right answers
hoping to please my parents
and get confirmed in the church.

When the minister questioned Mary
about her faith in Jesus
Mary told him she loved Jesus
because Jesus loved everybody

but she hated the crucifixion
because the crucifixion gave her
nightmares.

When the minister gently tried
to explain the crucifixion to her
she said, "I respect your explanation
of the crucifixion,
but I feel the Good Samaritan
speaks the message of Jesus
more than the crucifixion
speaks the message of Jesus."
"Why?" he asked her.

"Because," she said,
"the good Samaritan
took time to stop
and help an unfortunate stranger."

The minister looked troubled by
Mary's view of the crucifixion
but she and I both passed the class
and were confirmed in the church.

There was something about Mary's mind
that made me respect her.
It was her awareness of essentials,
what makes things the way they are,
and our classmates
recognized and respected
her insight.

When I was fourteen
I wanted to take Mary
to a school dance.
My Mom told me
she wouldn't drive me and Mary
to the dance
but she'd drive me
and our neighbor Lucy
if I asked Lucy,
so I didn't go to the dance.

Mom didn't like Mary.
I wasn't sure why back then.
Now I know
Mom didn't like Mary
because Mary's parents
were from Russia.
It was the Cold War era
when Russians and Americans
were taught to hate each other
and Mom, being born in America,
was suspicious of Russians.

Thinking back on
my Mother's fear of Russians,
I'm glad our church wasn't like Mom.
Our church kept the doors open
to all people regardless of birthplace.

In our last year of high school
Mary was elected president of our class.
She was in charge of
the annual used toy drive
collecting and distributing
used toys to people
who couldn't afford toys
for their children.
She asked me to help her.
I helped her load toys
in my Dad's new car.
Mary had a clipboard
with a list of names
of the valley's poor people.

One of the people on the list,
Mrs. Snow,
lived in a one room shack
beside the river on the edge of town.
I carried a doll house
up to the woman's door in the hot sun.
Mary told Mrs. Snow
the school sent us
with toys for her children.

Three skinny children in torn clothes
looked up at us.
Mrs. Snow held a baby
in her arms
and looked interested in the doll house.

Then, with a trace of fear in her shy voice,
she asked us if we wanted
a drink of water.

Mary respectfully thanked her
and told her we had to go back to school.

Mrs. Snow's worried look
troubled me.
I stopped the car by the river
and asked Mary
why Mrs. Snow
seemed uncomfortable with our visit.

With that look of wisdom
everybody respected
Mary said,
"Mrs. Snow is galled
by her poverty
but she's afraid of looking needy.
She's graceful
asking us if we want water."

In the rear view mirror
I saw a kite sticking up
from the pile of toys in the back seat.
I asked Mary
to help me fly the kite.
While we assembled it
on the grass beside the river
I asked Mary if she still had nightmares
about the crucifixion of Jesus.

She said when she had a nightmare
about Jesus on the cross
she'd wake up
and think about the Good Samaritan.

"The Jesus I know," she said,
"lives in people
who don't lord it over anybody
and love everybody."
I asked Mary,
"What if Mrs. Snow
told you Jesus would give her little girl
a mansion in heaven?
Would you go along with
Mrs. Snow's idea
of a mansion in heaven?"

Mary didn't answer my question,
she just asked me,
"Would you go along
with anybody's religion
just to keep them
from suffering?"

I told her, "Yeah,
that's how I'd like to be."

Looking like she was briefly entertained
by some pleasing thought
she asked me,
"Are you a pantheist?"

"What's that?"

"Do you see God in everything?"

"Yeah, I guess," I told her.

When I got the kite assembled
she was holding
the ball of string.
"Ready?" I asked her.
She held the ball of string
behind her back and said,
"If you want it
you'll have to get it."

I grabbed both her arms
but she held on to it.

I pulled her down
on the grass
and she rolled on top of me
pinning my arms down
on the grass.

I could have overturned her
but I just told her,
"You got the best of me
but I can still outrun you."
We used to foot race
when we were little.

We stood up
and flew the kite
soaring
back and forth
back and forth
across the sun
while we laughed
and felt good and noble
on our way to deliver
goods to the valley's poor people.

Before we graduated
Mary resigned her position
as class president.
She resigned to protest
the firing of our science teacher,
Mr. Lambert.
Lambert was a free spirited atheist
in our small, conservative Christian town.

After Mary and I graduated
I didn't see her for ten years.
Then when I returned
visiting home in the valley
I saw her in a supermarket.
She looked older and tougher.

She had new squint marks
around her eyes.

She was teaching history
in high school and said she loved it.

I asked her if she remembered
Mrs. Snow, and she said,
"As long as there are Mrs. Snows around
I'll always feel a bit of the cross
weighing on me."

Another twenty years went by.

Again I ran into her
on a visit home.
She'd become the principal
of the high school.

She was a widow.
I was single.

I took her out to dinner.
It was our first and only date.

In the night
I drove her up to a view point
on the valley rim
high over our hometown.

We talked
and reminisced.

She remembered the kite
from thirty years before.

We kissed.

I held her close
and felt our bodies and hearts
showing little wear
considering all the time
that had gone by
since the time we'd wrestled on the grass
in another life many years ago.
It seemed both of us had aged
to feel more tender affection.

She was living
with her son and her son's wife.
So when I drove her home
we sat outside kissing in the car.
We didn't want
to carry the scene inside
and make a bad impression.

Mysterious Friendship

Walt was my Father's friend.

After my Father passed on
Walt called and told me he wanted
to talk with me.

I drove over to his house.

With a grateful look
he thanked me for coming
and he said he wanted
to tell me a story.

He said that all his life
from childhood on
he'd felt a mysterious friendship
with people.

He said it started in school
when he felt
a mysterious friendship
with classmates.

Then when he was in the army
and marched with fellow soldiers
he felt a mysterious friendship.
"I've never told anybody this," he said,
"but I want someone
to know my secret
so the secret won't die with me.

The enemy captured me.
They gave me food
and blankets
so I wouldn't freeze in the snow
and I felt with them a mysterious friendship.

"I escaped from the enemy,
found my fellow soldiers
and went back into another battle.

"I found a wounded enemy soldier
and took him prisoner.
I shared my food and water
with the prisoner.

We found words to communicate with
and when we talked
I knew
that without a war
we could have been friends.
I can still feel it now,
a mysterious friendship.

"This has been my secret
for many years.
I've been ashamed
for feeling my enemy
was my friend.

Let my shame die with me
and tell my story
when I've passed on."

Walt passed on
a few months after that,
leaving me
to tell his tale
of mysterious friendship.

The Reason is Love

Little agitations
aggravated my deeper wounds
of loss and failure.
I hid the hurt
in a solitary life.

I had a temper.

It almost felt like
chaining myself in solitude
was protecting people
from myself.

I changed
when I met you.

You changed me
into a contented person
able to appreciate.

You changed me
with your attractive face
and your interesting personality.
You changed me
with gentle things you say and do,
gentle things
like that time
you were sitting
on the doorstep
working a crossword puzzle.

You looked up
and saw where I'd cut my forehead
on a swinging door at work.
You asked me
to bring you the antiseptic.
You saw the cut
as a chance to share
some time with me.
There on the doorstep
you cradled my head
in your arms
while you gently applied antiseptic
and kissed my lips.

Your gentle habits
inspire me
to try and be like you
so I can give you pleasure
you give me.

In the grocery store
I see apples.
I stop and scan them
knowing the color you like.
I select the right ones for you
wanting to give you something
the way you're always giving
things to me,
gentle things
like this wristwatch you gave me.
It's durable and accurate
like your personality.

It's always here
touching my skin
like thoughts of you
are always touching my mind.

I remember the occasion
when you gave me this watch.
It was my birthday.
In a way
this watch symbolizes
the birth I experienced meeting you
and learning about your good ways,
the birth I experienced
when you touched me
with your gentle hand
and I saw good intentions in your strong face
healing wounds I suffered before we met
and you told me
I healed wounds you suffered before we met.

We've given each other
the gift of healing.
What better gift is there
when the reason for the gift
is love.

Alone Together

Alone together
you and I
have our own country,
consistent affection
far away from
people with contrary moods,

our own wealth,
loving words and looks,

our own competition,
each of us trying
to give the other
more pleasure,

our own retreat
from the world of humdrum routine,
we escape into each other,

our own adventure,
seeing in each other
a voyage to a new harbor
relished for its exotic lure,

our own creed,
love and be loved,

our own bliss,
enough bliss
to make everybody
living and dead
want to join in.

The Spirit of Water

On the riverbank
I stand relishing the river,
the river flowing
among autumn trees
with their many colors.

How did I discover
this view of the river
with tall trees decorating it?

My friend Richard and I
made the discovery together.
When he visited me
he wanted to buy fresh peaches
to take back home to his family and friends.

Looking for peaches for sale
we followed rural roads
while we discussed ideas
our affection lit up.

We searched on
surrounded by peach orchards
glittering in the afternoon heat
inspiring us to ask each other,
"Isn't the river nearby?"
That's how I discovered
this view of the river in splendor.
Without my friend
I probably wouldn't have discovered it.

After he returned to his home
with his ripening gifts for friends
he sent me a gift,
one of many gentle gifts
he's given me over the years,
a picture he took of me
standing on the riverbank.

When I look at this picture
I imagine his gentle voice saying,
"Friend by the refreshing water."

Thanks, Richard,
because of you
I'm standing here on the riverbank
among majestic trees
on fire with gentle beauty
decorating our home,
the earth and sky.

We've shared many journeys
inner and outer,
making discoveries along the way,
discoveries like this river,
a nurturing god.

Because of you
I can stand here
and feel
the spirit of water.

Apples for Mrs. Jones

When I was a child
our next door neighbor, Mrs. Jones,
used to stand on her weedy lawn
looking around
taking things in.

Her messy, gray hair,
her clothes all black
and her loony expression
made children afraid of her.
Being afraid of her,
some of the children
threw rocks at her
and called her a witch.

Though I was afraid of her,
there was something in her
that drew me to her.
She wasn't like other adults.
She didn't seem to lord it over children
and she didn't seem in a hurry.

One day on my way home from school
I walked by her
and she smiled at me.
I'd never seen her smile.
I said hello to her
and she turned away
like she was afraid of me.

Sometime after that my Dad
told me she wanted me
to mow her lawn.

He could see the idea
made me nervous
and he said, "Don't be afraid.
She won't hurt you."
So I mowed her grass
and when she gave me a dollar
I saw deep suffering in her eyes
and wondered why
she looked so sad.

She pounded on our door
one night in a storm
when my new puppy was howling.
Dad opened the door
and she looked at me
with a tender loving look
and told Dad,
"The puppy's howling
from loneliness.

"The scent of your child's shirt
will comfort the orphan."

I took my shirt off,
laid it down,
and the puppy slept on it.

The strange woman's concern
for my dog
made me begin to trust her.

When I walked home from school
in the rain
a car stopped beside me.
It was her
motioning with her hand
for me to come into the car.

When I climbed onto the passenger seat
she wiped the water
off my face and hair
with the sleeve of her wrinkled black shirt
and with a soft voice
she told me I reminded her
of someone she used to know.
Then she looked at me
like she was afraid of me
and I tried to make her feel comfortable
by thanking her for taking me home
in the rain.

Back home I told Dad
she'd given me a ride home
and he said, "Here, take these apples over
and thank her."

She didn't answer the door,
so I left the apples on her porch
and didn't see her for many months.
I asked Dad,
"Where is she?"

"Before you were born
she had a son who died
when he was your age
and she's afraid
she'll love you like him
and you'll be taken away like him."

"Here," he said,
"take more apples over.
Sometimes you have to
keep trying.
Patience
is what holds your soul together."
So I went over there,
and when she didn't answer the door
I went around back
and knocked on her back door,
then I went back around front
and knocked on her front door
and called,
"Mrs. Jones! Mrs. Jones!"

She came out
and knelt down
and I felt her messy, gray hair
like springy wool next to my face,
and she tickled me
and held me in her arms
and kissed me.

After high school
I left home
and moved to a new city.

When I returned home for visits
I'd always go over to see her first thing
and we'd get caught up.

Though she passed on a few years ago
she still visits me sometimes
when life is rough,
the sleeve of her black shirt
gently wiping raindrops
off my shivering face,
and I recall my father's wisdom
like a flower
opening in the sun.
"Patience
is what holds your soul together."

Music

I'd been out late at night
with school friends
when my Father met me at the door.

"How are your studies going?"
he gently asked me.

I told him I could use more time
for studies
and he asked me,
"Why do you spend
so much time with your friends?"

I told him,
"I hear a kind of music
with my friends.
It fills my soul
like stars fill the sky."

He said, "That's good,
but you need to spend more time
filling your head
with your studies
so you can learn about truth
and do well in school."

And I told him,
"When I'm with my friends
it feels like we're on a pilgrimage
to learn the truth
and smile with it.
And with my friends
I feel the truth is love
like music in me and you
and everybody."

And he said,
"I used to be like you.
My Father, your Grandfather,
told me to channel my love
into work
so civilization becomes music.

"I tried,
but the world
made me suffer over
broken dreams
before you were born.

"With you I felt
my creation for the world is music
in harmony with the universe.
I labored for your safety
and I've tried to raise you
with values to outlast your pain
where dreams might not work out.

"Live and be happy.

"As much as I want to tell you
be careful
and reason your way
through life
I take joy in your joy.
I celebrate
the love you feel
like music in me and you
and everybody."

Hope

How can you see me
crazed with longing for you
and feel I'm giving you back
the love you give me?

To think before we met
I would walk singing
on a high hill
and feel my body alive
with strength to soar
like an eagle,
and now I'm falling
weak and low
bending to your desires
and loving the chance to please you,
my face like a mirror
of your smiles and frowns.

I can only hope
there's truth in the saying
"People who love
are people who deserve
to be rewarded by love."

And I can only hope you feel
that my love for you
somehow qualifies me
even though I feel
you're better than I am.

Like a Key to a Door

Jim's philosophy
was an interesting mixture.
He said that all together
the religions and philosophies
might make a key to a door.

That was Jim.
He was a cool thinking philosopher
and he was a warm feeling person
with a kind idea
to help anyone
in a quandary.

He was always there
when I was troubled,
always there
as if he was afraid
something might hurt me
and I loved him.

I remember
a conversation we had
before he passed away.

I'd been puzzling over
the nature of egotism
and had ended up with a dark view
of human nature.
I told Jim
some philosopher said,
"All the world over
each loves their own self the best."
I told Jim the thought seemed logical
and that it bothered me.

Jim wasn't particularly religious,
but he said with a proper tone
as if he had an answer,
"The human race is egocentric
and the Christian prophet knew
the human race is egocentric.
That's why he said,
'Love your neighbor as yourself.'"

Jim's recognition
that someone was trying
to fix human nature
made me feel a little better.

But there was something else bothering me,
and sensing Jim could make me feel better,
I told Jim some other philosopher
had said, "No two people
can be together
for more than a few minutes
without one trying to
establish an aristocracy over the other."

And Jim said,
"As a kind of cure for condescension,
here's a thought you might want to try on,
'True love
annihilates
the egotism of the heart
that politeness merely disguises
or suppresses.'"

That was Jim.
always looking for a solution.

Finally I told him,
"I guess the thing that really bothers me
is that I feel those philosophers
are describing me
when they talk about selfish people
wanting to lord it
and I feel disgusted with myself."

"O," he said with a tone that told me
he loved and respected me,
"Well here's another thought
you might want to try on.
This one came from somewhere back there
in the seventeen hundreds.
'Vice, prejudice, and ignorance
naturally cling to the soul,
and only idealistic conversation
can rescue it.'"

Jim ended our conversation
with another observation,
"You know," he said,
"I think back on the times I've suffered.
The sharp pain never lasted long,
and sometimes it gave over
to moments of ecstasy.
That's a comforting thought,
a good gift for the human race,
all suffering brings with it
a cure,
it just takes patience."

"Thanks for being patient with me," I told him.
"Your patience is a cure
I'm grateful for,"
and I laughed feeling better.

Seeing me laugh,
he laughed.

That was Jimmy.
He believed all the ideas
from all the philosophies and religions
were like a key to a door.

Life in the Universe

Lying on the beach
all white with sand
I watch a mother
with her little boy.

With a tiny red shovel
the boy digs
beside the ocean.

Several feet back
from the water
his mother is packing up
their beach things
while the boy calls pleading,
"Mom, let's stay!"
and she calls back to him,
"It's time to leave!"
while she slowly folds up
towels and beach chairs.

Occasionally she stops
what she's doing,
gazes at the ocean,
gazes at her child.
The boy keeps digging.

Diverted from her plan to leave
she kneels beside him
helping him dig a hole,
becoming like him
with no purpose
except to have fun
digging away
in the sand
while she grins
and goes along with
whatever's happening.

Their haphazard bliss
calms me.
I feel glad
they enjoy the gift
of loving and being loved.

The murmuring ocean
relaxes me.
my heavy eyelids
begin to shut out the world
while a soft breeze
takes me drifting away
toward another gift of life,
nurturing sleep.

Opening my eyes
I look far away
to the waiting horizon
where tomorrows
will bring the common goal,
and who knows?
I think Socrates said something like,
"Who can say
that death's long sleep
won't turn out to be
life's best gift?"

Turning my palms up,
I feel the sun
with its affectionate light
warm on my hands and face.

The woman and child
have packed up to leave.

Walking by me,
they both wave
as if our time together here
has made us companions
enjoying life in the universe.

I wave back.

The New Light

When we met, I told you
I'd been scarred.

You told me
a person's mind
lives in a house
that lets in a new light
through cracks
made by time.

When I knew you better,
I learned the new light
is your tender insight.

With you I learned
to see what I used to be,
a dim person
stooped over.

With you I became
what I am now,
a new person
standing in the sunlight.

There I see
life's messengers
in those neighbor children.
Celebrating joy,
they laugh and play with their dog.

There I see tall trees
decorate the street
for bold travelers.

Holding your hand,
I touch the great person
you've made of yourself
and I admire you
for coaxing me out of
the cold house of my past.

With you I see and feel the world
in a new light.

Travelers from the Dust

It was a low point in my life,
maybe the lowest,
my mid twenties.
I had no job.
and no skills to speak of.
A woman left.
Rent was due.
Sometimes I woke in the morning
looking forward to going to bed that night.

Then one morning
I saw in the paper
Chris Walker was going to sing
in a city a couple of hundred miles away.

I'd seen him sing
seven years before.
He sang songs
about love and loss,
faith and doubt.

He didn't try to posture himself
as some kind of hero,
just a person talking with people.

When I'd seen him sing
I'd felt he was my friend,
so, seven years later
I drove two hundred miles
to see him again,
and when he sang his songs
I felt his friendship
even stronger than before.

I felt so drawn to him
I found my way to his backstage dressing room
so I could try to be near him.

People were coming and going
laughing and drinking.

I told his guitar player
I'd driven a couple hundred miles
to see the show
and the guitar player yelled
at a group of people across the room,
"Hey Chris,
this guy drove two hundred miles to see the show!"

Chris called back to him,
"O, that's all I need to feel, guilt."

When Chris said he felt guilt
I realized from the sincere tone of his voice
he didn't think he was worth someone driving
two hundred miles to see him sing songs.
He slowly walked over
to where I was standing
and looked at me
like he wanted to ask me something,
but he could tell I was shy,
almost afraid of him,
so he wasn't sure how to approach me.

Then he came closer
with his face close to mine
since the room was noisy with people yelling,
and he said gently,
"Why did you come?"

"I don't know why.
I saw you a few years ago
and your voice, the look in your eyes,
something in your songs,
I don't know."

And he said, "Let's sit down here
and think about this.
Maybe we can figure it out."

When we sat on the couch
a reeling woman waving a bottle
spilled beer all over his pants.
He laughed and reached out his hand
to keep her from falling over.

We sat there for a couple minutes
before he said,
and I think we both realized this
at the same time,
he said to me,
"I think you came
because you want to feel
unconditional love
coming from me to you."

I confessed to him,
"Just now
I was thinking the same thing."

He thanked me for coming
and said he had a hard time
giving himself respect or love
and that I'd given him a gift
by coming to him.

The guitar player I'd spoken to earlier
staggered by and fell on us.
Chris grinned pushing him back up on his feet.

Then Chris looked gently in my eyes and said,
"But you didn't want to just hear the songs,
did you? You wanted me to tell you
I love you, person to person."

I bowed my head and confessed,
"Yes."

He said he was glad
to give me what I came for.
He hugged me
and told me he loved me.
I hugged him back.
A woman came
and told him he had to be interviewed
for some magazine
and he left.

I never saw him after that.

I went on with life
and through the years
I heard he'd burned out
and quit performing.
Then he was killed in a car wreck.

I won't forget him
taking time
to sit with a scarred soul
needing something he had to give.

And when I think of his face,
his calm eyes and sincere voice
singing his message to the world
and talking to me with that same gentleness
I recall a line from one of his songs,

"Love those who love you, fool."

Waters of Joy

Old friend,
I'm remembering
that hot afternoon
you called asking me to come over
to visit you and your family.

I had plans with my girlfriend
so I asked you,
"Could my girlfriend come?"
and you said gently, "Sure, bring her."

It was a hot day.
I left the car running
with the air conditioner on
when I picked up my girlfriend.
We both wore white shirts
and white pants
hoping our clothing would reflect the sun
and keep our skin cooler.

At your house
we found a note on your door
saying you'd be back soon.

We felt grateful
you'd left your door unlocked
so we could sit in your cool living room
next to the air conditioner.
When you returned
with your wife and daughter,
your daughter saw
the guests in white clothes
and said with an amused expression,
"O for a second
I thought the angels
had come to sit down in our house."

We all hugged
and when I pulled you close
my old friend,
I felt the supporting good will,
humor, and optimism
of friendship from childhood.

Later you took us all celebrating
with dinner at a restaurant
where the wine made us boisterous
and after dinner we apologized to the waitress,
"I hope we're not too loud."
"No," she said trying to sound polite,
"you're fine,"
and we left an extra tip
hoping nobody complained.

Outside there were street musicians
singing and playing guitars.
I heard their message
in the blessed coolness of the night,
"This is your home, the universe.
The universe loves you."

And though we sat down
on wooden benches
to quietly listen,
I felt we were all dancing together
shouting in the sky.

All those times…
I think back on
all those times
I've visited you
when you and your family
opened the door to your home,
and with the doors to our hearts open
I saw and experienced
a deeper, wider, loftier world
celebrating the greatness of life.

With gratitude and love
I look back
on those times,
especially that day
the sky scorched us
and together
we found an oasis
with each other
drinking the waters of joy.

The Wedding Dance

The week before we got married
my fiancé cooked dinner
for me, our best man Larry,
and the minister of her church,
Reverend White.

Sitting around the table
Larry and Reverend White
talked about religion
and the laws of our nation.
Larry told Reverend White,
"All policemen
should be members of a church
and when a policeman
arrests a criminal,
he should tell the criminal,
'Mend your ways
or punishment will come from God
in the afterlife.'"

With a respectful tone
Reverend White said to Larry,
"Your idea is interesting, Larry,
but with your permission,
could I express another
point of view?"

Larry looked surprised
by the minister's shy, respectful tone,
a tone without authority,
and Larry said to him,
"Yes, I'd like to hear
your point of view."

And Reverend White said,
"Conscience, if taught and developed,
is sufficient punishment from God
and the church should be kept
separate from the nation's enforcement
of the nation's laws."

Larry looked disappointed
because he liked the minister
and wanted the minister
to agree with him.

When Reverend White saw
Larry's disappointed look,
he told him, "I like you Larry.
You have a good heart."

After dinner, Larry helped my fiance
wash dishes and clean up
while I walked outside with the minister,
and while we looked up at the stars
I asked him, "Why does Larry
want the police to tell criminals
God will punish them?"

Reverend White said he thought
Larry had doubts about
whether there is a God
or a heaven or a hell
and Larry was trying
to dispel his doubts
by wanting the police
to express the view of the church.

When Larry came out drinking wine
he slid his arm around Reverend White
and told him, "I love you.
You're not a know it all.
You've kept your sense of shame
even though it's your job
to preach sermons."
And my fiancé standing by the door
said, "He keeps his sense of shame
because he believes
the purest wisdom is a loving heart
and he always feels ashamed
because he thinks he doesn't show
enough love for people."

Larry hugged Reverend White.

At the reception
after the wedding ceremony
I overheard Larry tell Reverend White,
"I want God
to work through me.
I feel like a lost sheep
wanting the shepherd
to lead me."

And the minister shouted
over the music,
"We're all lost sheep
until we find each other
and God is
everyone we meet!"

Larry drained his wine glass,
waved it around and danced.

The Artist

Telling me she loved me
she took my face
in her hands
and while she looked gently
into my eyes
I felt those hands,
her hands
touching me
with tender warmth
I'd never felt.

I told her,
"Nobody ever touched me
like you.
You're an artist
with your hands.
How do you do it?"

And she said,
"An artist's skill
isn't in their hands.
It's in their mind,
the way they see the subject."

So I asked her,
"What do you see in me
that makes you touch me
like you touch me?"

And she said,
"What I see in you
is love."

Richard

I think about my friend, Richard.
We've had some great conversations
accepting and acknowledging
each other.

I knew him casually
when we were classmates
in high school.
We spoke in the halls
calling each other
by our first names.

Those were the years
of trying on roles
wondering how to cast
ourselves in life.
He seemed to have cast himself
in the role of goodwill ambassador,
friend to humanity
even way back then,
and I tried to respond to him
with the same friendliness.

We didn't know each other
well enough to talk intimately,
but many years after high school
I moved to a city
we now live in
and we became true friends
with the memory of ourselves
as young people
in the dawn of our lives
casting a light
over our lives now.

It's a light that makes us feel special,
a light that gives us
optimism and hope
and belief,
belief in the thing
people cherish most,
the last thing people can be deprived of,
a desire to improve.

So in middle age
we became
in our conversations
young in spirit
describing to each other
our experiences
with women, jobs,
failures, successes,
and quests for meaning.

Talking with him
I felt accepted and acknowledged
and I tried to give him back
the same acceptance and acknowledgment.

I guess the word
I'd use to describe
the face he shows me is
openhearted.

When I was moving
from one place to another
he told me I could
stay with him
and his wife and children
in their house.
I didn't take him up on it,
not wanting to impose
and maybe endanger our friendship,
but I remember the way
he opened his door for me
and I think of it as a symbol
of the way he opens his heart for me
and I open my heart for him.

I don't think there's been a time
since we began confiding
when I felt anything
was too secret to tell him
and though I know
that no two people
can always agree,

he always shows me
a polite face
when he disagrees with me
and I try to do the same
for him.

He had a career as a teacher.
He taught thirty years.
He began his career
teaching government.
Some call government
the highest principle
of civilization.
He later taught creative writing
showing students
how to express themselves
and feel more alive with expression.

I imagine he gave his students
what he gives me,
the gift of feeling
accepted and acknowledged.

I'm sure he left the gift
in their hands.
He says there were times
a student wouldn't respond to him
but Richard would persist
and would feel rewarded
if he could give
an estranged student
an appreciation for life.

I think of the way
an ancient poet described love.
He said love is to be learned
by reaching out again
and again,
overcoming rejection
and heartache
until the prize is won
as surely
as you can see your face
in a mirror.

And what is Richard's
prize of love?
He lives in other people.
With him
people have a memory
of someone there
accepting and acknowledging,
someone saying,
"With your thoughts and feelings
you can understand life.
You can cry over it
and celebrate it."

Thanks, my friend.
Because of you
I feel more alive.

A House in the Sunrise

On an early walk
before sunup
I pass by dark houses
where people are sleeping.

Here and there
a streetlight dimly shows
the way back home.

And there
over the house I live in
I see
the moon.

The moon.

It's been up there so long.

And it will be up there
for so long.

Hey Moon,
do you care
what I do?

It doesn't matter
if the moon cares.
Down here below
on the earth
people have a stake
in each other.

The door to the house I live in
is beginning to appear ahead
with the sun rising up behind me.
I turn for a look
and see her
gently lighting the street.

I can even sense her
gently touching my face
with her warm hands,
such a friendly gesture
here between the eons,
the sun coming
out of cold darkness.
She brings the day's heat
and lights the world
so her people can see it.

A Welcome Grin

My neighbor
left her baby girl with me.
For another two hours
I'll be babysitting.

Feeling neglected
and doomed
the little girl
is wailing for her mother.

Can I fill the void
in this empty world
and somehow
stop those teardrops?

Maybe her bottle will help.

Holding her
in one arm
I use a free hand
to get the bottle
at the right temperature.
She wails louder.

Ooooooo!
Going hungry
is rough.

Here we go,
here's your warm bottle
but
what the…?
you're so distressed
you swat it away.

Here, let me clean your face
where milk
dribbled
down
your chin.

Now let's try again.

There,
the bottle's in
and that mouth
wet with tears
becomes a welcome grin.

She takes it all down.

We rest in peace.

Her contented look
lets me understand
why an Asian philosopher
called the infant
"The uncarved block,
a symbol of hope
for beauty."

Cradled on my arm
she looks contented
with contentment.
She's a good model
of peace and tranquility.

I hum a song for her.

She responds
grinning
and waving a hand.

Barry

After high school
I left home
and shared an apartment
with my friend Barry.

Barry loved books
and classical music.

He was five years older.

I looked up to him.

He was always asking me
to read lines he'd selected
in a book.
Then he'd ask me
what I thought about the lines
and when I told him what I thought
he'd say with a respectful tone,
"I see what you mean."

And he was always asking me
to listen to a piece of classical music.

He'd stand up
and wave his arms
pretending to conduct.
Raising his voice up
over the music
he'd say, "Isn't that beautiful!"
like he knew in his heart
it was beautiful
and he hoped I liked it.
I grew to love
many of those pieces he would play.

Neither of us had much money
from our jobs,
but with him
I had some of the best times
of my life.
He steeped himself in beauty
wherever he could find it,
books, music, people.

I rarely saw him drink or carouse.
He was more interested
in the books piled up
around his bed
and his chessboard.
He was always playing chess
and he loved
talking with people.

He'd try to understand
the inner world
of the person he talked with
and he'd make them feel
he accepted them.

The more I knew him
the more I tried
to steep myself in beauty
like him.
With his desire to seek,
to understand and celebrate,
he became like a guide
for my soul.

During the time
I lived with Barry
I had a girlfriend.
She lived a few blocks from us.

I loved her
and wanted to marry her,
but she left me
and her leaving broke me.
Barry told me
she'd made a mistake leaving me.
"It's her loss," he said,
and I was grateful
he tried to comfort me
but I had to get away
from there.

I moved to another city
to make my way alone
and forget her.

The world looked better
in a new city
but I still felt ashamed
and defeated.

My soul
Barry had led me to
was like the sun
with clouds obscuring
the face of the sun.
I fell into a routine
working like a cold machine
blind and deaf to people.

I tried to forget Barry
because he reminded me
of her
and the lost paradise
I shared with them.

I haven't seen him
for many years.
Sometimes I feel an urge
to locate him,
then I think no
it still hurts.

But the other day
driving down the road
I heard on the radio
a piece of classical music
he used to play.
It was a piece he taught me to love.

I felt a surge
of the old feeling
like he was there telling me,
"Carry this music in you
and become a vessel of beauty."

I recalled
one of his favorite poetry lines,
"Love survives
disappearing life."

Enough time had passed.

I called him.

He's even more beautiful now.

We're like before,
even better with age.

Friendship

My long time friend,
though we're now living
in different cities
you visit my mind
and I always feel grateful
you've come.

I look forward
to seeing you in the flesh
and talking with you.

With our shared sorrow
and shared joy
strengthening us
let's keep exploring
the river of life,
lashing our boats together,
lying back in revelry,
floating on.

May we always
adventure together
and hunger for more.

Car Wash

Waiting for the city bus
to take me to work
I sit on a wooden bench
reading a newspaper.

Suddenly
a young girl screams out something.

It's coming from across the street.
A girl maybe seven or eight
stands on a bus stop bench
and shouts at the traffic,
"Get your car washed!
Get your car washed!"

Another girl maybe ten or eleven
stands on the corner a few yards away
from the girl on the bench.
The girl on the corner holds up a sign,
CAR WASH
$5

On the corner
beside the girl with the sign
several girls are gathered
with buckets, rags, and a garden hose.

Cars slow down
to see what the shouting
is all about,
but nobody stops.

I get back to reading the newspaper.

Suddenly
it's all of them, all the girls
screaming together.

Somebody slows down
and turns the corner
stopping there
beside the girls with their buckets.

Hoping for a customer,
the girl on the bench leaps off
and runs to the car.

Two elderly women
climb out of the car
for a parley.

They discuss the transaction
with the girls…

deal complete.

The girls hug and dance around
shouting and celebrating.

The bus rolls in
and as I climb on
the bus driver asks,
"What's going on over there
across the street?"

"Car wash," I tell him,
"they just landed
their first clients."

He snorts,
shoves it in gear,
and we head on
down the road.

The Hippocratic Oath

I was standing in the hotel room
a half hour before
my niece's medical school
graduation ceremony.

Tired from an all night flight
the night before
I was having trouble focusing
on the necktie.
Taking a couple of tries
to tie it
I thought
this must be what it's like
growing old,
losing your ability to cope
as you approach death,
then dying while others are born.

I thought about my niece.
Here she was graduating
from medical school
and my strongest memory of her was
when she was a baby in my arms
and her mother would say to me,
"She likes you better than most,"
and I would cradle the child
and feast on her tranquil gaze
and whisper, "Hi Melissa,"
and meditate on
the Asian religious symbol
of mysterious wisdom, love, and peace,
the infant.

As Melissa grew older
there grew between us
an unspoken bond that seemed to say,
"Regardless what we see in each other,
there's something underneath it all
that means the same thing."

Wanting to look presentable for her
and her boyfriend I hadn't met
I inspected myself in the mirror.
Clothes?...they'll do.
Face?...looking tired from no sleep.
An ancient monk known for wisdom
said his wisdom consisted
of only two things.
One, sleep at the right time.
Two, eat at the right time.

I ate an apple
and took the elevator down
to meet my brother and his wife
in the lobby.
He's a doctor and his happy eyes
told me he felt good
having his daughter with him
on the same path.
I inspected my brother's tie.
He's three years younger
and I had to watch over him
when we were boys.
Through the years we've maintained
a tactful reserve with each other.
There's a saying, "Friendships depend
for their duration on tactful reserve."
His tie needed tightening.
I didn't say anything
but my hands reached up
without thinking
and straightened my brother's tie.
He thanked me.

I walked with my brother
across the parking lot
to the auditorium
where he introduced me
to Melissa's boyfriend.
The boyfriend's face
reflected awareness and good will
that made me feel
he's a fellow traveler.

A faint sound of bagpipes
echoed through the auditorium.
One of the doctors on the teaching staff
walked slowly toward the stage
playing the bagpipes
and leading a long line
of medical students down the aisle.

The students wore black robes
like the German custom of the 1800's
when the doctors, lawyers, and clergy
all wore black robes,
a symbol of their mourning
the suffering of the human race.

A woman medical student
spoke with a friendly voice
into the microphone
delivering the invocation
with phrases like, "Let us serve
more than we ever dreamed of.
Let our faces always reflect
the good will of our hearts."

After she spoke, others spoke,
doctors, the dean,
then the keynote speaker, a TV newsman,
said the most inspiring people he'd interviewed
weren't famous statesmen, athletes, or entertainers.

He said the most inspiring people
were the doctors
in poor countries
and on forgotten battlefields.
The speaker ended his speech
with the story
of his best friend from childhood
dying of terminal cancer.
His friend wanted assisted suicide
but when his friend got used to
the thought of dying
he decided to have a birthday party
with friends and family
and his friend is still alive
savoring the days.

After telling the story
of his childhood friend,
the speaker ended his speech
by challenging the new doctors,
"Teach us how to live
and how to die,"
and everybody gave him
a standing ovation.

A doctor on the teaching staff
stood playing a guitar
and singing a song with the message,
"If some experience makes you bitter,
set your heart right,"
reminding me of an ancient poet's message.

"The great challenge of life
is to never step off the path of love,
not for one second."
Then their names were called out,
and one by one each student
walked to the stage
to receive their diploma
while a doctor draped a red and yellow sash
around their shoulders
and the audience applauded.

When my niece Melissa walked up,
I remembered holding her
and rocking her.
I felt a strange sense of loss
like life was slipping
through my fingers,
slipping away
like water
through my fingers.

Taking a break from the ceremony
I caught sight of my face
in the bathroom mirror,
worn but still hopeful,
carrying decades
of good and bad memories.

There's a saying,
"Good memories lose their sweetness,
bad memories keep their sting."
If that saying is true,
what hope is there for contentment
with the past?

Gratitude must be the answer.
I cupped running water from the faucet,
drank deep to quench thirst,
and walked back to the auditorium
alive with fellow travelers.

The ceremony was ending.

The dean of the medical school delivered
the Hippocratic Oath,
"We will do no harm,
and we will heal impartially
all members of the human race,"
thoughts written two thousand years ago
by a man in Greece.

Then the doctor with the bagpipes
led the new doctors
in black, red, and yellow
out of the auditorium
while the sound of his music
faded away.

Outside by a pool of water
with a fountain,
we watched the new healers
walk out of the building
to mingle with family and friends
in the crowd.

With a shy look
Melissa came to her father,
and they both smiled.
It felt good to know
she's on the path
he's been on for many years,
the path of
the Hippocratic Oath,
always being there to heal.
He gave her a long hug,
and when he released her,
I told her, "My turn,"
and she laughed.

Walking and talking
with her and her boyfriend
on the way back to the hotel
I confided to them
that earlier that morning,
when I'd felt tired from the late night flight
I'd imagined how it must feel
to be older and fatigued by long life
and walking in the shadow of death.

With a compassionate look
her boyfriend said,
"It's something we all go through,"
and with her same childlike tranquility
from long ago
when I rocked her in my arms
she said, "How could
something like death be bad,
something so necessary and natural?"

A Beautiful Lady

I'd been jilted.

I'd heard time heals wounds
but as time went on
the pain got worse
and I was beginning to feel
I'd have to bear up with it
the rest of my life.

My Mother knew
my heart was broken.
She knew I was turning my back
on the world.
She was hurting for me
but my wound was so deep
I didn't feel strength
to comfort her.

I overheard her on the phone
telling my Father,
"Of all the people I've known
our son has the lowest self image."

When she got off the phone
I asked her,
"Mom would you rather
I talked with a sense of shamelessness
or a sense of shame?"

She bowed her head thinking.

"Mom, I'm just trying
to make you feel better."

Wiping tears from her eyes she said,
"If you were shameless
I'd feel I failed you as a Mother.
But I don't want you
to always feel shame.
I want you to be happy enough
to feel good with people."

I told her, "I can feel good with people
when I have energy
to try to come across
in a good light for them.
If I'm with people
and can't please them
I just feel guilt."

She said, "You and I are probably
a lot alike.
If everybody had my conscience
nobody would feel righteous
or proud of being a good person.

"I say the wrong thing
and leave the right thing unsaid.
But I am your mother.
I always will be.
And I want to ask you a personal question.
Could I?"

"Yes," I said with affectionate obediance.

"Do you still love her?"

I didn't say anything
but my mother knew.

"It's not your fault," she said,
"you didn't plan it.
It just happened.
Time will heal this."

"I don't know," I told her,
"It seems time is making it worse.
And I'm starting to give up hope
it'll get better."

"It'll get better, she said.
Life has many parts
and this is just one part.
A part is not the whole
and you have years ahead of you."

"Thank you for telling me that,"
I said trying to sound congenial.
She frowned sadly like she knew
my melancholy face
was a tiny shadow
of the vast darkness inside me.

She gently hugged me
and I cried telling her, "I'm sorry for
putting you through this."

"I love you," she said.

"I love you too.
You're the most beautiful lady
I've ever seen."

"Will you come to the table
for supper?" she said softly.

"Yes, I said with determination
to come across in a good light for her.
And in time I found
what she told me was true.

A rough road isn't the whole journey.

Brother

My friend Richard
has a gentle dog
always friendly,
always anxious
to see me.

Richard named the dog
Brother.
Brother is a good name
for a family dog.
Brother's family
is the human race.
He loves everybody.

When Richard and I
sit in lawn chairs
discussing our lives,
our ideas and feelings,
Brother pushes his soft face
into my palm
and gently licks
as if asking me
to stroke him.

Brother's affectionate manner
is so calming
I feel him lulling my mind
away from conversation with Richard.

Sometimes Richard becomes
almost a background
to Brother
while I lean forward
stroking Brother's soft head
with both hands
and running my fingers
through his golden fur
all the way down his sides.

So I go back and forth,
listening to Richard's peaceful voice
soothing my mind
with his beautiful ideas,
and then with Richard's voice
like Brother's accompaniment,
I focus on the gentle loving creature
at my feet,
a creature I can easily carry to heaven
with the touch of my hand
and follow him there.

Canoe on down to the Ocean

My Dad was a good Father
well respected
in the company he worked for,
but for me
the canoe symbolized him.

He built it in the back yard.
It was his dream
to build something
that could take people
adventuring.

He was working on his dream
in the back yard
while I played with a neighbor boy,
Miles.
Miles had a BB gun.

We found an infant bird
fallen from a nest
and Miles said with a tone of wisdom
like he was sure of himself,
"I'll kill the bird
before a cat kills him."
I told him, "No,"
and he said, "Why not?
The bird will just kill
worms and grasshoppers.
We'll save them by killing the bird."

There was a tone in Miles voice
I always distrusted after that.
It's the tone of self righteousness.

When he raised his gun to kill the bird
my Mother stepped in front of him,
took the bird in her hands and stroked it
while she called Dad
and Dad left his work on the canoe
to return the bird to its nest
in the tree.

Several months later
when Dad finished the canoe
he asked me if I wanted Miles
to run the river with us
and I told Dad no,
there was something about Miles
that upset the way
the world should be.

A few years later
when I got my first driver's license
I'd drive alone to the river
to work on canoeing skills.
My dream was to someday
take a girlfriend or a wife
adventuring.

But I spent too much time on the river
and Dad got upset with me
for neglecting my homework
so I quit practicing the art
of river running.

I missed the river
so I felt glad
when Dad planned a river trip
for Mom, my little brother, me,
and my girlfriend Lana.
He drove us all
through the hot day
to the boat dock.

When we were loading up
my mother screamed
and we saw my little brother
slipping off the dock
and falling into the river.

He didn't know how to swim.
He was sinking,
his face tilted back
looking up at me,
his arms reaching.
He was holding his breath
by some instinct
nature had given him
when I dived in
and pulled him out.

My father was proud of me
for the rescue
and Mom kissed me.

Later my girlfriend Lana
whispered to me,
"I love you.
That's all I need to know
for as long as I live."

I told her I loved her,
but I knew that I didn't know
what love is
and I wasn't sure if I felt it.

When I graduated
Dad wanted me to get a job,
so I joined the army.

Dad had served five years
in the army
and he always spoke respectfully
of soldiers.

Mom didn't want me to join.
She said armies can murder
and nationalism
is just sophisticated tribalism.

In officers' training
I was assigned to a company
with my old neighbor Miles.
As upperclassmen
we had the right to
outlandishly command underclassmen
and to deny them food in the mess hall.
Miles nearly starved
one of the underclassmen named Griffin.
One night I heard Miles
shouting with his tone of authority.

I looked out the barracks window
and saw him taunting Griffin.
He was making Griffin
crawl on his stomach on the gravel.
I went outside and told Griffin
to get up
and go back to his company.

He was so thin and weak
he could hardly stand up
and walk away.

Miles scowled at me.
It was a malevolent scowl
that made me want to kill him.

Miles made people feel like hell.
And I knew
that as long there were people like Miles
there would always be hell on Earth
and that a person like him in power
might turn a whole country evil.
But as much as I hated him
I knew he sent money home every month
to his poor mother and invalid sister.
So I had to admit
there was a part of Miles,
his love
for his unfortunate Mom and sister,
that reminded me
of my best friend in the company,
Chris.

Chris never tormented underclassmen.
He was always helping lagers
and sweeping and picking up
in the barracks.

When we graduated
I hugged Chris and told him
I'd miss him.
We gave each other
our parents' addresses
to help us track each other
in the future.

After graduation
I went home on leave
to see my parents.

Back home
everything looked foreign.

The army had become my new home.
My old home, childhood,
had become like a foreign country
far away from home.

I shook hands with Dad
and kissed Mom,
but I couldn't feel them.
I was acting like a son
and behaving properly,
but there was some unseen force
watching me,
ready to correct and admonish me
if I made a wrong move.
It was fear
the army had implanted in me.

That first night I was home
I eavesdropped on Mom and Dad
talking in their bedroom.

Mom said,
"He's lost his sincerity
and friendliness.
There's something missing from his heart."
And Dad said,
"He's less affected and more purposeful,
taking pleasure in responsibilities."

Maybe they were both right,
but whatever I was,
it was something different
from what I was before the army.
What I was before the army
was gone.

I hadn't talked with Lana
for almost a year
but I called her anyway
looking for a part of me
that was lost.
She told me she'd met someone
and was getting married.

She told me I'd been
her first love
and she thanked me
for showing her what love is.

I realized
I hadn't experienced love
like she had
and I wondered
if something was wrong with me.

We said good bye
with a formal tone.

I wandered through the house
looking for signs of what I'd been
and there in the garage
I saw the canoe.
It looked strong and sturdy,
but I had no urge
to take it on the river.
Another part of me was dead.
I leaned my head against the wall.

My Father came out
looking for me.
He told me he was proud of me
and asked if I needed anything.
I told him no,
but he saw something wasn't right.

He told me he was glad
I was in good health
and alive.

He said one of his friends at work
had lost a son in the war
and I could see my Father
trying to make me feel compassion
to take away my own pain.
It's a lesson he always taught.
It works.

I walked with him
back into the living room
and saw my little brother
there on the couch with his girlfriend.
He looked ecstatic
and I knew he'd found love.
He beat me to it.
And I wondered again
if there was something wrong with me.

He looked up at me
like he was in love with everything
and he told me he wanted to
join the army like me.
Mom said no with anger in her voice
and I remembered him
sinking down in the river
when he was a little boy.
I walked over to him,
put my hands on his shoulders,
pulled him up off the couch
and hugged him.

It was the first loving emotion
I'd felt in months.
"Go to college," I told him.
"Skip the army."

It's not that I disrespected soldiers.
I'd known noble soldiers,
but I was afraid my little brother
would encounter a soldier like Miles
and Miles would warp him.

My brother looked up in my eyes
like he idolized me.
I felt like I had two faces,
the face of my Father
defining the soldier as noble,
and the face of my Mother
defining the soldier as
a legalized murderer.
The longer I was home on leave
the more upset my Mother seemed.
I could see she was driving Dad away
with her disappointment in me
losing my gentle manner
of childhood.

Though I tried to show affection
she could see
my affection was well meant
but insincere.

I moved on to my next station,
a two year assignment stateside.
I'd been there a year
when Chris called.
He'd been my best friend
in officers' training.
He'd served a year in the war
and come back stateside.
He said Miles had been killed
by somebody in Miles's own company.
They couldn't find the murderer,
too many suspects.
Everybody wanted Miles dead.

I asked Chris how he felt about
the cruelty of army training
starving us physically and caging our minds.
He said our training had cut him away
from his past
and made his old childhood home
seem like a foreign country.
He said that when we were underclassmen
with our heads shaved,
our faces gaunt,
our bodies weak,
he had a vision
that we'd all died
and were passing through a limbo
to something else.
I asked him if he felt hatred
for what they did to us.

He said he felt
the world mishandled us
but that he was letting go
his hatred
so he could pass out of hell.

"Into heaven?" I asked him.
He laughed and said, "Why not?"

I told him I loved him
and to give my love to his wife.

After serving a three year term
in the army
I moved back
into civilian life.
A few years after the discharge
I found Emily,
She was my first love.

I took her home
to meet Mom and Dad.
We stayed for a week.

That first night
after Emily had gone to bed
Mom said with affection,
"Emily's a beautiful person,"
and Mom hugged me
like she'd found something
she'd lost.

She could see
I was happy.
With affection she'd shown me
when I was a child
she told me she loved me
and I kissed her.

After Mom went to bed
I told Dad I noticed
Mom drank a whole bottle of wine
at dinner.
He said she started drinking
when I went into the army.
"The wine," he said,
"makes her feel
the universe
is unfolding
as it should."

After talking with Dad
I went to the garage
to check on the canoe.

It was still there
ready to take me and Emily
adventuring.
The next morning
Emily and I took the canoe
to the river dock.

I saw a thin, mangy coyote
across the river.
He chased a duck.
The duck flew evading the coyote
and I felt deep pity
for creatures
always scavenging
and evading each other.

I asked Emily
if she ever felt sorry
for animals
scavenging all their lives,
all their lives
living in fear
of predators.
She said, "You don't see them
in their moments of awareness.
Maybe their plight
strengthens the peace they feel
in the nest or the lair."

I wondered about
the order of things,
people self absorbed,
countries self absorbed,
even galaxies
eating each other,
and why?

I asked Emily,
"Why is everything
preying on itself?"

She said,
"The way of death
makes life.
It all exists
for its beauty.
It's a gift."

I recognized that thought,
"It exists for its beauty."
The thought
was already a part of me
before she said it.

I realized I was parts of her
and she was parts of me
the way I was parts of
everybody I'd known
and they were parts of me.

My first girlfriend Lana
telling me I taught her to love
was part of me.
I was part of Lana
learning to love.

With Emily in the bow
we floated in peace.

I imagined death
was just a bend in the river,
maybe a section
of exciting rapids.

"Hey," I said to Emily
to get her attention.
She looked back.

"I love you,
and that's all I need to know
for as long as I live."

She grinned
and turned back
looking ahead.

More Love Tomorrow

Admiring your gentle insight,
trusting the way you act on kindness,
overcome by your charm,
I feel our conversations are adventures.
We adventure with each other
talking about our lives.

With you I look beyond my guilt and failure
so I can celebrate people in my past
and feel grateful they loved me
and I loved them.

You tell me about your life,
and I feel honored and grateful
for your honesty and your trust.
Thank you for telling me about
the people in your past,
now people in my past,
your fears, now my fears,
your hopes and dreams,
now my hopes and dreams.

The thought of you and I together
tomorrow and always
makes me want to always be a loving soul
you've made me into,
a loving soul like you
while the past disappears with yesterday
and our love grows ripe today
for our harvest of
more love tomorrow.

Affairs

I'm a lover
carrying on many affairs
at the same time,
all the affairs
with you.

I have an affair
with your eyes,
beautiful,
innocent,
interested,
accepting,
tranquil.
I look in your eyes,
and it feels like I'm disappearing
in you
and becoming more alive with you.

I have an affair
with whatever it is
that gives your eyes
mysterious beauty,
whatever's in your heart and mind.

I have an affair
with your humble tone of voice
that doesn't lord ideas
over people.
You hold things in suspense,
the mark of a good person
not approaching things
with preconception.

I have an affair
with the way you touch me,
your fingers gentle on my skin,
the way you lock your fingers with mine
making me feel I'm closer to you
and what's inside you.

I even have an affair with
your clothes,
the way they gently touch your skin.

I have an affair with the way you walk,
simply, gracefully, slowly,
not hurried.

I have an affair with
the way you talk gently with people,
and I imagine the gratitude
they must feel to know you.

I have an affair with
the way you seem to use
all you know
to make me love you.

I have an affair with
the way I use all I know
to make you love me.

I have an affair with
the way you make me
into a better person
because I try to anticipate you
hoping you love my sensitivity enough
to love me
for what I am to you.

I have an affair with
the way you whisper,
"I love you,"
when I hold you close
and kiss your lips.

I even have an affair with
the way you make me worry about you
when we're not together.
You even make me love
the pain of love.

I have an affair with
the way you wonder
if you've done enough for others,
your conscience
that makes you wonder if you're good
when you see bad.

I have an affair with
the way you educate your will
to accept and respect.

I have an affair with
the way you pick out
the good you see in people
and you don't let the bad
infect your way of loving them.

I have an affair with
the way you make me want
to be with you,
an affair with
the bliss I feel kissing you,
an affair with
the way you make me feel
grateful seeing you,
grateful knowing you,
grateful thinking about you.

I ask my heart and mind
for the strength
to enjoy what we have together
without trying to possess you
and I ask for the strength
to let you go
if you must go.

I love you
with passion that scares me,
then, loosening its grip,
makes me feel free and strong
and proud for knowing you,
for knowing you care enough
to spend time with me,
and for knowing
that because of you
people seem better off
for knowing me.

You change me into
a more loving person,
and the bounty
spills over to them.
Let them drink and be satisfied.

Jim

Trying to wake from sleep,
in between sleep and waking
I felt sleep was death pressing in on me.

Waking I wondered what's wrong?
and I realize again,
death has taken you, Jim.

With your beautiful soul
you gave joy to my life
and now you're gone
I walk around silent and sad
all day long.

What'll I do
if I get tired grieving you?

I don't know.

Sun in the sky,
you saw us
walking and talking together
and you probably wondered
why we spent little time
talking about wine, lust, trinkets.

You probably wondered
why we gave ourselves
to the search for ideas,
ideas I loved, Jim,
because they linked our minds.

River running through our hometown
didn't you see us walking beside you
all the time?
Was there ever a time
you didn't see us
talking together on our joyful search
for meaning?

And now the water has flowed away
to the ocean,
the ocean vast like the soul
of my friend.

His large soul stooped
to give meaning to a body here.
His soul was high
like the heaven he's going back to
and his soul was low
like the low water of the river.
His soul was high
with noble aims
and the skill to act on them.
His soul was low,
so low
that it made room for me.

He was after knowledge
and when he learned something
his knowledge seemed like it had
sought him out
so he could express it
with his beautiful gift of words.

And he was fun.
He could joke
without forgetting
to respect peoples' values.

And whenever a wise idea
came into the conversation
he always acknowledged it
even though his own searching mind
had similar notions written in it
as if he'd been born that way.

Mary and the Lion

When I was a child,
the teachers told us to sing
"Mary Had a Little Lamb"
and we sang it,
but I never thought
about the meaning of the song.

Many years later
I saw the lyrics
in a book my wife had saved
from her childhood.

When my wife saw me reading the lyrics
she impressed me with her memory
of the song's gentle message,
"The lamb
followed Mary to school
because Mary
loved the lamb."

Many more years went by,
years with conflict and peace,
years with pleasure and pain,
then I came across the song lyrics
to "Mary Had a Little Lamb"
on the wall in a used bookstore.

On the same wall
above the lyrics
there was a large picture
of a lion.

When the man behind the counter
saw me reading the song lyrics
he quoted some of the lyrics.

"The lamb," he said,
"followed Mary to school one day.
It was against the rule.
It made the children laugh and play
to see a lamb at school."

I asked him
why he nailed the song lyrics
underneath a picture of a lion.
"Something to think about," he said.

I told him the lion and lamb
reminded me of a definition of reality,
conflicting wills.

And the man said,
"A person will always run into
peoples' opposition
unless the person goes to live alone
in the wilderness."

Then he sang a couple of lines
from another song the teachers taught us
way back in childhood,
"Home on the Range,
where seldom is heard
a discouraging word."

We both laughed.
He praised me for
my sense of humor.
I thanked him for his ideas
and told him
he'd let my thoughts
feel at home
ranging around
with Mary and the lion
and the lamb.

"Good," he said,
"it makes me happy
to be able to give
the gift of ranging around
without going anywhere.
That's freedom.

And freedom can even outshine
what may be
the greatest happiness of the human race."

"What's that?" I asked.

"Hope," he said.

Friendship Set on Fire

The friendship I've imagined
and always wanted
I only find with you.

When I'm hurt
I won't be a prisoner to pain
as long as I can think about you.

When people I believed in
no longer want me there,
I can face my mistakes
with new hope to improve
when I think about you.

Your kindness
keeps you from shrinking away
when impatience makes me scowl.

When faults weigh me down,
you have the sensitivity
to not bring them up.

You know my admiration for you
makes me vulnerable.
Still your character keeps you from
hurting me when your patience is tried.
When I look back on my life
I see mistakes I'm ashamed of,
but I've learned from the past
what most deserves my praise.

It's you.

On the bare land where I thirst,
your gentleness is a fountain.

A feeling that I'm talking with
the highest part of my soul
is a feeling I can only get
when we talk.

The friendship I've imagined
and always wanted
I can only find with you.

It's from you I've learned
love is friendship set on fire.

The River

See the many colored rocks
glimmering under the surface
of the clear flowing river.

I imagine the river
telling me she's happy
flowing clear and untroubled
so I can see her stone jewelry
there below her clear surface.

In my mind
the river's kind voice
confides with me.

"I want to satisfy you," she says.
"Even when I wait behind dams,
even when I cross deserts,
I still find my way to you
so I can quench your thirst.

"If you wonder why
I want to satisfy you,
my ancestors,
the raindrop and snowflake,
made me the way I am.

"As for my brothers and sisters,
the rivers of the earth,
we can be dangerous
when we swell up and flood,
but the best part of us
wants to please you
until we give up our lives
and join the great water.

"Come,
let me wash your feet
and refresh your body."

Following the river's voice in my mind,
I take off my shoes
and let her soothing water
refresh and purify me.

I want to ask her
if she knows how it feels
to join the great water,
but her voice in my mind
has flowed on with her,
leaving me to experience bliss
from her soothing touch.

Her graceful kindness
inspires me
to make my own ending
to her story.
She joins with the ocean
like a person in love
disappears into
another person love has made
into a welcoming home.

The Meaning of Life

Some say
the meaning of life
can be revealed with words.

If the meaning of life
can be revealed with words,
then you are my language.

And with you as my language
I find the meaning of life
is love.

Sunlight

Walking through the rain
I smile with you
and celebrate the rain
now that we've both
come from lonely years.

To think
you and I
felt this same rain
on our faces
before we knew each other
and I felt
the touch of your hand,
warm like your gentle heart
that gives your face charm.

With a look of affection
on your charming face
you lock your fingers in mine
and we see among rain clouds
a rainbow
like a messenger
letting us know
the sun is on its way.

To think
you and I
felt the same sun
on our faces
before we talked
and your appreciating thoughts
lit my life.

To think
we walked
through this same world
with years alone
wrapped like chains
around our separate bodies
and we didn't know
love was coming
to break us free
from those chains of loneliness
and turn us loose together.

Epilogue

Because you're the best
of my life
I feel we share
a life
in life
like an affair
in a valley
of the world
where a river
finds its way
to refresh our bodies
with water
and a way
to quench our thirst
for peace.

Afterword

Thank you
for taking an interest
in this book.

When I first learned
how to write
I imagined you there.

Over the years
I began to feel you
as real as my hands
and my eyes.

With your attentiveness
making room for me
you became
what I imagined
you to be
when I started.
You are beauty
made real.

Acknowledgements

My first acknowledgement
is to you
for taking an interest
in these words.

Taking interest
in words from another person
sounds simple,
but it's not all that common
for someone
to get outside their own skin
long enough
to consider what another person
thinks and feels.

If your life is like mine,
you were gently handled at birth
when you were taken
into the world's light,
but as you grew older
you got hammered
and shaped
on the anvil
of civilization.

Not only have you endured
the trials
your good character
has prevailed
with your desire
to open yourself
to another person's
thoughts and feelings.

I'm grateful to you
for reading this.

I'm also grateful
for people
who guided me to you.

Without them
I wouldn't have met you.

I'm grateful for
publishers Richard Weekley
and Dr. Karunesh Agarwal,
and the Book Excellence Organization,
grateful for inspiration they
and others give with kind words
to make people feel
at home in the world.
I'm grateful to all of them
for guiding me to you
with their calling
to reach out
with friendly optimism.

When I think of them
I see them
like you.

They, like you,
are the best
of what I try
to deserve.

They honor me
with their gracious wisdom
and attentiveness
guiding me
among tall mountains
where we search for ways
to live up to you
and to come across for you.

You're the inspiration
on the journey.

About Steve Jackson

Steve Jackson is an internationally published poet. His poems have appeared in *The Salmon* (Ireland) and a multitude of literary magazines around the world.

Both his first and second books of poems, *Wade in the Water (2005)* and *An Affair in the Valley: A Collection of Poems* (2014), were published by the *Los Angeles Poets Press* founded in 1982 by Richard Weekly and Jerry Danielson with their aim "to bring buried works to the light, to the surface of the earth, and to the hearts of the receptive."

His third book of poems, *The Harbor* (2019) was published in New Dehli, India by Dr. Karunesh Agarwal, managing editor of the *Taj Majal Press* and *Cyberwit.net,* whose missions are "to bring the world's best poetry to the world."

Books by Steve Jackson

An Affair in the Valley:
A Collection of Poems

An Affair in the Valley:
A Collection of Poems
is the story of
a person's road through childhood
and into the new world
beyond those early years.

It's a road where a person can fall
scowling alone in the dust.

It's a road where a person can walk
and laugh with an understanding friend.

On this road a person can feel perplexed
by someone's customs
until good intentions are sensed.

With sincerity,
the face of a soul,
people can rescue hearts from hate
and make each other feel
peaceful,
caring,
and fearless
in this brief time in eternity
where the sky
gently holds the world
in her arms.

An Affair in the Valley
describes a person's road
as a road passing through
sorrow and rapture,
sorrow
for people confined in darkness
by cruel, intimidating walls,
and rapture,
rapture for people
with a liberator
opening a door
to the sunlight
where the world
is common ground
for all breathers.

The liberator in the book
is anybody
speaking a kind, respectful word
leaving its image
on another person's heart.
The liberator is an outer sign
of inner affection
making all people
one family in the stars.

The Harbor

The Harbor is a collection of poems
about people facing dark trials
with strength to turn wariness
into peace, love and hope.

It's a book about people
with unfinished business,
people still heroic enough
to make room in their heart
for another person.

The book is about bold acts,
beautiful, random acts
where a helping hand
is like fire to comfort
a chilly person anguishing.

The book is about affection
and admiration
animating a person's body
with an adventurous soul
turning crisis
into opportunity.

The Harbor
is a book is about people
armed with love so fearless
it lets the mind's voice whisper,
"Even death will have an exit door."

And like a person in rapture
the atmosphere of this book
seems to say,
"Where the road ahead
disappears
in chilly darkness,
look again.
The cordial world
not only waits up ahead
with her graceful gift,
sunrise,
she's already here
with a great gift,
the gift of you."

Wade in the Water

Wade in the Water
describes existence
as being like a rose.

Though people may suffer
getting cut by thorns
and withdrawing alone
in cold silence
where nothing is heard or seen,
everything still carries a message
like that flower.

A mother
soothing a restless child,
a snail
carrying its home
on its back
while it climbs
out of flooded grass,
tears for the pity
of war,
a child comforting a mother,
people with scars healing,
the sky
gently and gladly
offering her sunrise
after a cold night,
life's events in this book
seem to speak a message
symbolized by a rose
over thorns.

Taking time to listen
and to see
a traveler in the universe
might feel victorious rapture
watching children
playing under a rainbow.
The children
living for joy and love
are like freedom's prophets
with their shared tears
and shared laughter
joining hearts
on a mutual quest.

Wade in the Water
describes the earth they play on
as being like one country
at peace
on common ground,
ground so common
a bold imagination might see it
like a great ship
on a journey
through the rain
and into the sun,
a great ship
born to carry her people home.

losangelespoetspress.com

stevejacksonpoems.com